Edith Can Shoot Things and Hit Them

by A. Rey Pamatmat

A SAMUEL FRENCH ACTING EDITION

SAMUEL FRENCH
FOUNDED 1830

SAMUELFRENCH.COM

ISBN 978-0-573-70016-3   Printed in U.S.A.   #28060

MUSIC USE NOTE

EDITH CAN SHOOT THINGS AND HIT THEM received its world premiere production by Actors Theatre of Louisville as part of the 2011 Humana Festival of New American Plays. It was directed by May Adrales; the set was by Brian Sidney Bembridge; the costume design was by Connie Furr-Soloman; the lighting design was by Jeff Nellis; the sound design was by Benjamin Marcum; the props design was by Joe Cunningham; the media design was by Philip Allgeier; the fight director was Drew Fracher; dramaturgy was by Michael Bigelow Dixon; and the production stage manager was Kimberly First-Aycock. The cast was as follows:

EDITH . . . . Teresa Avia Lim
KENNY . . . . Jon Norman Schneider
BENJI. . . . . Cory Michael Smith

CHARACTERS

(in order of appearance)

EDITH – 12, Filipino-American, a girl, Kenny's sister
KENNY – 16, Filipino-American, a young man, Edith's brother
BENJI – 16, any race, a friend

SETTING

A remote non-working farm outside of a remote town in remotest Middle America.

TIME

The early 90's.

AUTHOR'S NOTES

Edith Can Shoot Things and Hit Them should be performed by young-looking adult actors, not actual teenagers.

Ed and Eddie are pronounced as the diminutive nicknames of the male name Edward.

The shadows in for Mother can be done with puppets, projections, or something else non-human. Please do not use actual people – NO GROWN UPS!

ACT I

Everyone says so

(In darkness a girl's voice hums "Ein Männlein steht im Walde" from Engelbert Humperdinck's Hänsel Und Gretel.*)*

(Lights rise on a barn with a rafter that intersects with a cross support firmly rooted in the dirt. There are a couple bales of hay and a haystack at its base.)

(EDITH sits on the rafter, 10-12 feet above the ground. She is 12 and wears a stained T-shirt, ratty shorts, and is barefoot. She holds a giant stuffed frog to which she is too old to be talking, but she does exactly that.)

EDITH. I am very mature for my age. It's true, Fergie, I am. I look twelve, but I'm really much, much older. Everyone says so.

(EDITH looks at the frog as though listening to her, pauses, and then punches her in the face.)

Who cares what you believe? The truth is true. Our kind mature at a different speed than stupid, little human girls. On my planet, I'm a full-grown grown up, and I have my own apartment where I live without my twenty parents. Who needs them?

(pause)

Yeah! Twenty people to build one baby, and they all get together to help the baby grow. Feed her and make her clothes and paint her bedroom a different color every month no matter how expensive it is. There's always someone around, because everyone has twenty parents.

EDITH. *(cont.)* But that was when I was small. Now I'm stuck here, alone on this planet as a test. To see – well, I don't know, but it's a test. THAT'S the test: for me to figure out what the test is. And I've got to do it fast, before the evil shape-changing aliens from an enemy planet take over our world!

And Kenny waits to see if I complete the test, which is how he'll know I'm ready to fight in the war. And when I am, I'll sprout wings and fly away! My kind have wings when they grow up.

(pause)

Well, I mean, I'm grown up now, but when I grow up more, I'll fly away and return to my planet, shoot those aliens in their faces, save Kenny's life, and rescue my twenty parents, who are really, actually helpless without me. And I'm going to do it all by myself.

And when I do, Kenny will stay home because he'll be so proud of me. For being such a big girl. A big, grown up girl. With wings.

End of Scene

Liar

(Moments later. KENNY enters and looks up to the rafter, where EDITH sits. KENNY is 16, a fairly average guy. The most outstanding thing about KENNY is the masterful degree to which he doesn't stand out. He's dressed to leave home.)

KENNY. You shouldn't be up there.

EDITH. When is he coming home?

KENNY. How should I know?

EDITH. He tells you.

KENNY. Not always.

EDITH. When I look out the barn door from here, I can see past the hay all the way into the orchard.

KENNY. Will you get down?

EDITH. Last time he was here, it was so annoying. I was practicing my song for choir, but he needed to sleep. He yelled at me, and I was all, "This is homework!" So I came out here, because he's a jerk.

KENNY. He didn't mean it. To yell.

EDITH. Yes, he did.

KENNY. Only because he was tired.

EDITH. So I came out here and sang and sang and sang until my head exploded. And it made me want to fly, so that's when I figured out I could get up here.

KENNY. Don't ever go up there when I'm not home.

EDITH. I'm not going to fall.

KENNY. But what if you do? You shouldn't even be up there now.

(EDITH tumbles like she's going to fall, but wraps her legs around the support so she just dangles upside down.)

EDITH!

(EDITH laughs.)

If you fall –

EDITH. I WON'T.

KENNY. Accidents aren't on purpose, that's why they're accidents, and if you have one, it'll take the police or an ambulance an hour or more to get here.

EDITH. Forty-five minutes. They'll do the sirens.

KENNY. Forty-five minutes is still too long if your head is cracked open.

*(**EDITH** makes a siren noise.)*

Get down.

EDITH. He was home anyway.

KENNY. Like that matters. He wouldn't have done anything. When you were little – when we were both little, there were termites in this barn.

EDITH. There were?

KENNY. An infestation of termites that ate through everything, and even though the wood looks fine, the barn isn't. It could fall. That rafter could break. You could fall. At any time.

EDITH. When we were little?

KENNY. Yeah. Yes.

EDITH. We didn't live here. When we were little we didn't even live here.

KENNY. They told us when we got the house.

EDITH. You're such a liar.

KENNY. Can you please come down?

EDITH. What do you think happens when you go out?

KENNY. What do you mean?

EDITH. Why won't your friend come here?

KENNY. We already have plans. I'm going to his –

EDITH. Benji's.

KENNY. His mom would freak.

EDITH. Why?

KENNY. No proper supervision here.

EDITH. He's sixteen. You're sixteen.

KENNY. She's over-protective.

EDITH. And we're under protected.

KENNY. I protect you.

EDITH. I can protect you, too –

KENNY. Which is why I want you to get down. Because I'm being over-protective.

EDITH. You just want to leave. And you don't want Benji to come over here, that's why you're leaving. And when you do, I'll just be here by myself and anything could happen.

KENNY. But it won't.

EDITH. You don't know.

KENNY. But I trust you.

EDITH. Make him come over. Stay here. There's nobody here.

KENNY. Ed…

EDITH. Kenny…

KENNY. Next time, I'll. I'll try to figure out something next time, if you climb down now.

EDITH. GET down. You can only climb up.

KENNY. I'll ask Benji. Get down.

(**EDITH** *considers. She gets down.*)

EDITH. What's for dinner?

KENNY. Spaghetti?

EDITH. Pizza. The long ones in the oven, not the micro-wave ones.

KENNY. We don't have any.

EDITH. Take me to the store.

KENNY. Okay, but we're walking.

EDITH. Why?

KENNY. We're almost out of money.

EDITH. He didn't put any in the bank?

KENNY. Don't worry. He will. He just hasn't yet.

EDITH. Drive me to the store, and I'll walk back by myself. And then you can just go on to Benji's from there. Or I can go with you.

KENNY. You're not walking at night for half an hour by yourself. We'll get you pizza and walk home together. Then I'll go. By myself. And you won't climb up there while I'm gone.

EDITH. Okay, but the long kind. On bread.

KENNY. Get your shoes on.

EDITH. Maybe you should call him.

KENNY. I left him a message.

EDITH. What if he doesn't call back?

KENNY. He will. And if he doesn't, I'll figure it out. I always figure it out, right?

EDITH. Mostly.

KENNY. There will be money in the account tomorrow.

EDITH. He'll forget. Just call. Call Dad.

End of Scene

Hunting for Gnomes

(**EDITH** *sits on the couch. The TV is on playing a movie like* The Gnome-mobile *on VHS. In her lap is 6th grade math homework. Next to her is a partly eaten French bread pizza. Next to that are a remote control, a cordless phone handset, and her stuffed frog.*)

(*The couch seems huge with her on it all by herself.*)

(*She watches TV. Does a math problem. Eats some pizza. Again.*)

(*Time passes. She's completely alone.*)

(*The phone rings.* **EDITH** *pauses the movie and answers.*)

EDITH. Hello?

Hey. I'm doing it now.

Invert and multiply.

You flip the numerator and the denominator. INVERT.

Dina, this is so basic. This is the review lesson before the actual lesson. This isn't even the 6th grade math part of 6th grade math.

I don't know why it works, it just does. Just do it.

No, I don't want to talk to your mom. Don't. Don't put her –

Hiiiiiii…I'm okay, Mrs. Osheyack.

My Dad's at work.

My brother's in the bathroom.

Pizza.

Okay, we'll eat healthy tomorrow.

I'm going to bed soon.

He's here; he's just in the bathroom. I'm completely safe. I can take care of myself.

Could you put Dina on?

I hate you.

I'll hang up next time. Tell her to worry about you. You're the one who can't remember fractions.

EDITH. *(cont.)* Invert. Multiply. Reduce. Then you're done.

Yeah, I'm going to bed now.

Okay. See you tomorrow.

*(**EDITH** hangs up. She looks around the room, pensively, and then turns to the frog.)*

We're completely safe.

*(**EDITH** re-starts the movie, turns up the volume, looks around again, and then exits.)*

TV.

Oh, we'll hunt for gnomes in the countryside,
Over hill and dale, both far and wide.
And we will not rest till we've found a bride,
A gnome who will stand at Casper's side.

Is that a gnome here? Or that a gnome there?
And when we find her will she care,
That Casper is handsome and true and fair,
So she'll happily be half of our married pair?

(As the TV plays, there is noise offstage. A door opening, some rummaging, maybe a trunk opening or a step stool unfolding.)

*(**EDITH** re-enters. In one hand she holds a hand pumped air rifle; in the other, a hunting bow and some arrows.)*

(She uses the remote to turn off the TV and exits the opposite side of the stage [and the house].)

End of Scene

Changing

(The next evening. The same couch.)

(**BENJI** *stands next to one end, clutching his gigantic book bag.* **EDITH** *sits on the other end scrambling a Rubik's Cube.)*

(**BENJI** *will one day go to MIT to become a civil engineer or to RISD to become an architect. Right now, though, he is too thin and too hunched over with hair that's a bit too long, clothes that are too starched, and aviator glasses that are too big for his face. He's 16. A classmate of Kenny's.)*

EDITH. Is it a sleepover?

BENJI. Just hanging out.

EDITH. No one's here.

BENJI. Why?

EDITH. No one's ever here but us. You could sleepover, and no one would care.

BENJI. There's school tomorrow.

EDITH. We go to school, too.

BENJI. My mom would worry.

EDITH. Tell her not to. It's safe here. I can shoot things. You're totally safe. I can hit stuff.

BENJI. Why would I...would you do that?

EDITH. Because it's true. We're well-supervised and pro-tected.

(**KENNY** *enters with a stack of comic books.)*

KENNY. *(to* **EDITH***)* Do your homework.

(**EDITH** *holds out the Cube.)*

EDITH. Do it.

KENNY. I'm not doing your homework.

EDITH. No this.

KENNY. *(to* **BENJI***)* You can sit.

(**BENJI** *does.)*

EDITH. Fix it.

KENNY. You mixed it up, you do it.

EDITH. I can't. Fix it.

BENJI. You can? Let me see.

(KENNY *hands* BENJI *the comics and takes the Cube.*)

KENNY. I'll do it, and then you'll go in the kitchen and do your homework.

EDITH. Okay, okay.

(KENNY *starts solving the Cube.*)

He's not really figuring it out. He uses algorithms. Do you know what that is?

BENJI. That is – they are set series of steps.

EDITH. Right. So if the cube looks one way, he does these steps. If it looks a different way, he does different steps. He doesn't know why he twists one side or the other. He just knows what will happen in the end once he completes the steps.

BENJI. That's still figuring it out.

EDITH. It's like, "If this, then that. If this, then that." Over and over till it's done. Like a computer following a program. He's like a robot. He doesn't even need to think sometimes. He just knows what to do and does it. Barely thinking. Just doing.

BENJI. How did you learn?

KENNY. I got this book and one weekend I just learned how.

EDITH. We didn't have gas, and there was no money left in the bank, so we were trying not to go anywhere.

(KENNY *has finished the first two layers by now.*)

BENJI. Wait. Is it done?

KENNY. Almost.

(KENNY *finishes the last layer as* BENJI *watches, fascinated.*)

There.

BENJI. Wow.

EDITH. Again! One more time.

KENNY. I'm not your monkey. Do your homework.

(*EDITH huffs and goes off.*)

BENJI. That's so rad.

KENNY. You could learn, too. She's right: I'm not thinking, just doing.

(*holds up a comic*)

This is it. Issue 20.

BENJI. Does it hint or does it show it?

KENNY. Actual, full on, lesbian kissing. There are these girls – Kathy and Lenny – and they're traveling across America with this alien guy, Shade. And Kathy's in love with Shade but also feels like she doesn't get him, because, you know –

BENJI. He's an alien.

KENNY. So she ends up hooking up with Lenny. Total girl on girl.

BENJI. You said kissing.

KENNY. Well, they show kissing, but they definitely do more. I mean, there's even an issue where Shade changes into a blanket.

BENJI. What do you mean?

KENNY. That's his power. He changes into things or people. So he changes into a blanket and Kathy and Lenny don't know, and they do it on top of him.

BENJI. Girl on girl.

KENNY. Yeah.

BENJI. Lesbian stuff?

KENNY. Yeah.

BENJI. Wow, that's so –

KENNY. YEAH. And there's one where –

(*EDITH comes in carrying her homework.*)

Kitchen.

EDITH. It's boring in there. I'm doing my homework. I'm just doing it here.

KENNY. *(to* **BENJI***)* Let's go to my room.

EDITH. NO. Stay here.

KENNY. We're having a private conversation.

(to **BENJI***)*

Or we could go to the barn.

EDITH. No. You're here, so stay here. I'll go to the kitchen. Just don't leave the house.

KENNY. Okay. We'll be there soon to make dinner.

*(***EDITH** *gets up and goes back into the kitchen.)*

BENJI. You can cook?

KENNY. Yeah. Okay, so there's this other issue where Shade changes into a woman. His power is out of control. And while he's a she, he has sex with this gardener.

BENJI. Who's a guy, I assume?

KENNY. Yup.

BENJI. So, it's like, gay.

KENNY. Not really, because Shade's a woman. But mentally he's a man, and he talks about how it feels having someone inside him instead of being inside someone else.

BENJI. Your dad let's you read this?

KENNY. He doesn't know.

BENJI. Can I read them?

KENNY. Yeah. Take them. I've read all of them.

BENJI. No. Can I read them here? My mom will freak if she sees them. She goes through my stuff, and if she misses stuff, my brother tells her.

KENNY. What a tool.

BENJI. That's what older brothers are like.

KENNY. I'm not.

BENJI. Not in general. But you are to Ed. A little.

KENNY. You said you brought something?

BENJI. I'll show you later. In the barn.

KENNY. No one's here.

BENJI. Ed.

KENNY. Ed doesn't care.

BENJI. I do.

KENNY. We can just go in my bedroom. She's not allowed in there. She knows I'd kill her if –

(**BENJI** *kisses* **KENNY**. *It's sudden but seductive.*)

BENJI. I'd rather go out back to the barn. Okay?

(**BENJI** *kisses him again.*)

KENNY. Okay.

End of Scene

Interruption

(A rotary phone. It rings.)

*(**KENNY** goes to it. **BENJI** reads comics.)*

*(**KENNY** pauses, readies himself, and then answers.)*

KENNY. Hello?

We're fine. We're about to make dinner. You know how Ed likes that Hamburger Helper with the macaroni and cheese? I figured there must be a way to do it with real cheese and –

Oh, sorry. You tired?

We will.

Wait. Did you put money in the bank last week? It didn't go through if you did.

Mostly gas, so we need food.

*(**EDITH** pokes her head in the room and watches **KENNY** on the phone, intently.)*

(in phone)

Well, I have to pick Ed up from extra-curricular stuff. Choir. And there's driving her to practice and voice lessons.

You got two months, after that I used the money in the bank. And we need food.

I will, but you missed a week.

Yes, you did, and we need food.

What should I do? Send her to Mrs. Osheyack's for the weekend again?

*(Yelling comes from the phone. **KENNY** takes it from his ear and holds it against his chest to quiet the yelling.)*

EDITH. What are you doing?

KENNY. Shhh. Wait one sec.

*(**KENNY** puts the phone to his ear again.)*

Sorry. I won't...sorry for my tone.

KENNY. *(cont.)* I'll budget better this week. I will. But we still need something.

Okay. How much?

(KENNY gives a thumbs up. EDITH is relieved.)

Okay. Ed's here, so –

Oh. All right. I'll tell her. Thanks.

Bye.

(KENNY hangs up.)

He's busy.

EDITH. Is he at work?

KENNY. No, Chloë's. But he has to rest so he can –

EDITH. I don't care. He paid for six months. Of voice lessons.

KENNY. He doesn't remember. He doesn't really know how much each month cost.

EDITH. Because you got them, right? You told him what to get me for Christmas, and you got them, right?

KENNY. Yeah. Anyway, now he'll put extra money in the bank, and we'll save it in case he forgets again.

EDITH. And now you don't have to tell him you used up gas driving to Benji's every night.

KENNY. We need the money.

EDITH. And now he's here, and you'll have to use more gas driving him home.

KENNY. You wanted me to bring him over, and I did.

EDITH. I know. I don't care.

BENJI. Um…Kenny?

(KENNY realizes BENJI has overheard their conversation.)

KENNY. Let's start dinner.

BENJI. Should I do something?

EDITH. Can you cook?

BENJI. No. I can…set the table.

EDITH. Table? We eat in the living room with the TV.

BENJI. Only barbarians watch TV while they eat.

EDITH. What?

BENJI. That's what my mom says.

EDITH. Barbarians don't even have TV. Where'd you find this guy?

KENNY. We're the only sophomores in Pre-Calc. Go in the kitchen and do your homework.

(to **BENJI***)*

Could you put those comics in my room?

*(***EDITH** *and* **BENJI** *go.)*

*(***KENNY** *looks at the phone. He hates it. He picks up the receiver, pauses, then puts it back down off the cradle.)*

(He disconnects the phone from the wall.)

End of Scene

Science

(**KENNY** *and* **BENJI** *in the barn, sitting in the hay.* **BENJI** *pulls a dictionary out of his bookbag.*)

KENNY. That's what you brought?

BENJI. Yes.

KENNY. I have a dictionary. You didn't have to carry that in your bag all day.

BENJI. But I marked pages.

(**BENJI** *shows him strips of paper that he's inserted between pages.*)

Pages with key words. Because they exist. Words...for what we do. Are doing.

KENNY. Doing when?

BENJI. You know when.

KENNY. But I want you to say it.

BENJI. Words like, fellatio.

KENNY. "Fellatio?"

(**BENJI** *turns to the page in the dictionary.*)

BENJI. *(reading)* "Fellatio. Noun. Oral stimulation of the penis."

KENNY. I already have a word for that. BJ. Blowjob. A word and an abbreviation.

BENJI. I know what a BJ is, thank you.

KENNY. Exactly. So why do we need a dictionary?

BENJI. Why do we need a comic book with lesbian kissing in it?

KENNY. Because it means that this stuff happens. People kiss people. Not just boys kissing girls or girls kissing boys. People just kiss people. And give them BJs.

BENJI. That's what I mean. There are words for it. And not just crass words or the words they use at my mother's church. These words…"fellatio" is scientific. It's not – there's no. It's not condemning people who do it, and it's not glorifying them either. No bias. There's a scientific word for it, because it is a scientific fact that it happens. And since it happens it needs to be named. And so it is.

(KENNY *kisses* BENJI.)

KENNY. What's the word for that?

BENJI. That's just a kiss.

KENNY. Just?

BENJI. How come we go to my house?

KENNY. I…don't know.

BENJI. Is your dad ever home?

KENNY. Not really.

BENJI. Where is he?

KENNY. Work. Or his girlfriend's. Chloë.

BENJI. So…

KENNY. It's embarrassing. He's never here.

BENJI. That's a good thing. I mean, no interruptions.

KENNY. Most of the time. But then he'll just suddenly show up. We'll come home from school and there he'll be, or he'll get off a late shift at the hospital and just show up here in the middle of the night.

BENJI. But most of the time –

KENNY. Sometimes I just. I want to leave here. That's all.

BENJI. Have you ever run out of money?

KENNY. A couple times. I just send Edith to Dina Osheyack's, and then all I have to do is fend for myself.

BENJI. How come your dad's never here?

KENNY. Look: can I fellatio you now?

BENJI. It's not a verb.

KENNY. So can I give you a fellatio now?

BENJI. It's an act, not an object. Were you even listening to me?

KENNY. Yes.

BENJI. You're making fun of me.

KENNY. Not really. A little.

BENJI. You will not be getting any fellatio today.

KENNY. Oh, really?

(**KENNY** *starts to rub* **BENJI** *through his pants.* **BENJI** *tries to stare at him, stonily, but is failing.*)

BENJI. There are...words. Other words.

KENNY. Like what?

BENJI. Homosexual. That's a scientific word. Not faggot – like burn the faggots. Or gay – like we're carefree and happy and gay. "Adjective. Of, relating to, or having a sexual orientation to persons of the same sex." No judgement. Just a fact. Homo-homosexual.

(**KENNY** *keeps rubbing, leaning in closer.*)

KENNY. Mm-hmm.

BENJI. And mutual masturbation. Frottage.

KENNY. What else?

BENJI. A...uh. There's, uh...

KENNY. What?

BENJI. Anal. Anal intercourse.

(**KENNY** *stops.*)

KENNY. Oh.

BENJI. Um, you know what that – ?

KENNY. Of course, I do. It's fucking, but...I mean, yeah. It's fucking butt.

BENJI. Right.

KENNY. Have you ever?

BENJI. No. I've never anything. Except.

KENNY. Fellatio.

BENJI. Blowjobs. Yeah. Have you?

KENNY. No. How could I have...?

BENJI. I don't know. I was just asking.

(*They sit quietly not knowing what to do with themselves.*)

KENNY. *(indicating the dictionary)* Is there. Is it in there? Anal intercourse.

BENJI. No. But I found a medical book.

(BENJI takes out a scrap of paper that he scribbled on.)

(reading) "Anal intercourse: the sex act involving insertion of the penis into the anus."

KENNY. That sounds. I mean.

BENJI. What?

KENNY. Pretty easy.

BENJI. Yeah. It also…it sounds. Very scientific. We could. Be like scientists.

KENNY. What do you mean?

BENJI. I did research, and we could be like scientists. We could do an experiment.

(BENJI pulls a bottle of lotion out of his bag.)

KENNY. Oh, an experiment…?

(BENJI kisses KENNY.)

BENJI. Only if you want to. You don't want to?

KENNY. I don't…know if I want to.

BENJI. Oh.

KENNY. But I want…

(KENNY kisses BENJI. He takes off BENJI's glasses and takes BENJI's head in his hands, staring into his eyes.)

(20 seconds.)

Okay.

BENJI. Are you sure?

KENNY. Yeah. Okay.

(They start to make out.)

BENJI. *(backing away)* If you were running out of money, why did you use up gas to come get me?

(KENNY reaches for BENJI and kisses him again.)

End of Scene

Keeping Watch

(Outside the barn.)

*(**EDITH** drags a metal bucket onstage. In her other hand her air rifle and bow. Under her arm is her giant stuffed frog. She flips the bucket upside down and sits.)*

EDITH. I don't know what's better, Fergie. Back to back? If we sit right up against the barn, we can sit next to each other and still have a good view of the surrounding area.

*(**EDITH** pulls the bucket further upstage and then sits on it facing slightly to the left. She positions Fergie next to her facing slightly to the right.)*

This is a very important mission, okay? Keep the intruder inside the barn, by any means necessary. Kill, don't capture, capice?

It won't be hard. Did you see that guy? He's the kind of guy who's allergic to something stupid like peanuts or corn or air or something. He would lose a fight with a mosquito. But that's no excuse to be lazy. He could be a shape-changer – part of the test to see if I'm ready for war! And even if he's not, we've got to be sure he doesn't make trouble. You know what happens when outsiders come here, right?

It's a good thing we're so good at this, Fergie. Because Kenny really isn't. He gets in a tough spot and he won't blast his way through, guns blazing. He doesn't even get himself into tough spots. He just walks around them. But to execute this mission – our mission – you have to stand up and face things and say:

*(**EDITH** bolts upright and points the rifle at someone.)*

"Hey! Who goes there?"

*(**EDITH**'s eagle eyes pierce through the night. After a moment, she relaxes and lowers the gun.)*

False alarm. Thanks for backing me up, though.

Hey, watch this. See the hay bale?

(**EDITH** *pumps the rifle and shoots. Sound of a pellet getting swallowed up by straw.*)

EDITH. *(cont.)* Pretty good, right? Okay, okay. Watch this. See the trash can?

(**EDITH** *pumps. Shoots. Sound of a pellet hitting plastic.*)

One more, one more. That leaf.

(*Pumps. Shoots. No sound.*)

Okay, well. I'm still good, though. I just need more practice.

Anyway, I don't know what Benji's deal is. So till we figure it out we have to keep a close eye on him. This is a very, very important mission, Fergie. Very important.

(**EDITH** *keeps watch.*)

(*10 seconds.*)

(*Lights change, indicating the passage of time.*)

(**EDITH** *has fallen asleep on the ground in front of the bucket. She hugs Fergie to her.*)

(**KENNY** *and* **BENJI** *enter, holding hands, and see* **EDITH**. **KENNY** *nods to* **BENJI** *who exits.* **KENNY** *wakes her.*)

KENNY. Hey. Ed. Eddie.

EDITH. *(sitting up quickly)* The mission!

KENNY. Edith.

(**EDITH** *sees* **KENNY**.)

Go in the house. I'm going to drive Benji home.

EDITH. I'll come with you. I have to keep an eye on him.

KENNY. He'll get home safe, I promise. Go to bed.

(**KENNY** *starts to walk off.*)

EDITH. I'm tired of being here by myself. You get to leave, but I'm stuck here.

(*a beat*)

KENNY. Bring a pillow. Lay down in the back seat and go right to sleep, okay? You can't be falling asleep in school tomorrow. You need to be well rested, okay?

EDITH. I'll use Fergie as a pillow.

KENNY. Okay.

(EDITH *tries groggily to stand. After a moment,* KENNY *picks her up.* EDITH *wraps her arms around* KENNY*'s neck as he carries her to the car.*)

End of Scene

Cleaning the House

(The living room. BENJI sits on the floor in front of the couch doing Pre-Calc homework. KENNY's book is next to him, but KENNY is not there.)

(EDITH, however, is. She watches him, her arms hiding something behind her back. After a few seconds, BENJI feels her eyes on him. He looks up at her.)

EDITH. You again.

BENJI. …Hi.

EDITH. Mm-hmm. You're always here.

BENJI. Studying.

EDITH. Why do you have to study so much?

BENJI. It's an accelerated class. We cover Algebra II and Trig in one class instead of two.

EDITH. It's still a lot of studying. You stupid?

BENJI. Is your brother stupid?

EDITH. No. He's almost as smart as me.

BENJI. Well, we're in the same class, so I guess I must be almost as smart as you, too. That's why we're study buddies.

EDITH. Is that all you are?

BENJI. I…I don't…what do you mean?

EDITH. He's never needed a study buddy before.

(EDITH takes her arms from behind her back. She holds her bow in them, trained on BENJI, who freezes.)

BENJI. What's that for?

EDITH. Nothing. Do you know Mrs. Osheyack?

BENJI. Mrs…what?

EDITH. Or Dina Osheyack? Her brother goes to your school.

BENJI. Tom Osheyack? He stuffed me in a locker when I was a freshman, because I wouldn't trade it for his. I hate that guy.

EDITH. Tommy did? Oh…so you aren't friends?

BENJI. Definitely not. Is that okay?

EDITH. I'm friends with Dina, and one time her mom drives me home from choir. And Dina's mom has to pee so bad, she comes in the house. I don't want her to, but she does.

And the house is a mess. She asks, "Is anyone here?" Dad is at work. Kenny is still at yearbook. She gets all weird about it. I show her how when I'm home I micro-wave food for dinner. Or, if I know Kenny is coming home fast, how I start the rice cooker. But it makes her even more upset, so she plants herself in the living room and waits till Kenny gets home. She even cleans the living room a little bit.

And then she keeps calling, for weeks after that, asking for my dad. And, finally, they talk. And then he yells at Kenny for not keeping the house clean, and then he yells at me for letting someone inside.

BENJI. Your dad sounds – that sucks.

EDITH. So Kenny doesn't really let anyone in the house anymore. And he cleans a lot.

BENJI. It is, yeah, really clean.

EDITH. But he let you in.

BENJI. Oh.

EDITH. Did Mrs. Osheyack hire you to spy on us?

BENJI. No!

EDITH. She's always in our business now.

BENJI. I don't even know her.

EDITH. Maybe Tommy paid you to trick Kenny, so you could –

BENJI. Tommy – Tom wouldn't be caught dead talking to me.

EDITH. Then why are you here?

BENJI. Because Kenny falls asleep in class.

EDITH. No, he doesn't.

BENJI. Yeah. Kenny missed the assignment one day and asked me what pages we were supposed to do for homework. Because he was sleeping.

EDITH. Doesn't he get in trouble?

BENJI. He did once. But he said to Mr. Eaton, "When I stop getting straight A's in Pre-Calc, then you can tell me to stop sleeping. But right now, my method is working fine."

EDITH. WHAT?

BENJI. I know. I was amazed. Your brother doesn't like adults that much.

EDITH. I don't, either.

BENJI. So anyway, we kept talking to each other when we didn't get stuff, and then we'd sit together, and then we were friends.

EDITH. You're hiding something. He talks about you all the time.

BENJI. No, I'm...oh. He does? Good stuff?

EDITH. Yeah. Ever since Mrs. Osheyack, Kenny says no one can know dad's not here, because they'll split us up. But here you are and you know. It's like you cast an evil spell on him. Or tricked him.

BENJI. Well, I didn't. I just...I'm studying. I wouldn't do anything to...get Kenny in trouble. Or you. Trust me. It's the last thing I'd ever want.

(10 seconds.)

(**EDITH** *lowers her bow.*)

EDITH. Okay.

BENJI. Okay?

EDITH. Yeah. I believe you.

BENJI. Good.

EDITH. Does Kenny talk about me?

BENJI. Yeah.

EDITH. All the time?

BENJI. He said you could sing really well. And he said you like ice cream. Butter pecan.

EDITH. And French Vanilla. But not regular vanilla. I don't know why.

(**KENNY** *enters with some snacks.*)

KENNY. Dad just called. He wants to know if you learned your music for tomorrow.

EDITH. Liar.

KENNY. Okay, I want to know.

EDITH. Yup. I did.

KENNY. So sing.

(*a beat*)

(**EDITH** *considers making something up and then relents.*)

Go learn your music.

(**EDITH** *sighs and exits.*)

Didn't mean to make you baby-sit.

BENJI. No, it's cool. Edith's all right.

KENNY. Oh. Okay.

BENJI. Don't worry. I still like you more. I talk about you all the time.

KENNY. Shut up. I don't care.

(**KENNY** *picks up his book and starts studying, as* **BENJI** *watches him, smiling.* **BENJI** *resumes studying, too.*)

End of Scene

Showdown

(**KENNY** *wears an open button down.* **EDITH** *wears her usual stained, ratty clothes. The rotary phone is between them.*)

(**KENNY** *puts his hands on his hips.*)

KENNY. You cannot wear that outside this house.

EDITH. I can do whatever. I. Want.

KENNY. Change. Your. Clothes.

EDITH. Make me.

KENNY. You really want that? Because I will force a dress on you.

EDITH. I'll tear it off.

KENNY. I'll glue it on you.

EDITH. You can't do that!

KENNY. I have this special glue that will keep a dress stuck on you for a week, and if you try to take it off, it will rip off your skin. So either put one on for a couple of hours, or plan on having one stuck to you for days.

EDITH. You're all talk.

(**KENNY** *jumps at* **EDITH** *and chases her around the living room, but she's far too fast.*)

I'll call the police! I'll tell them you touched me in an area covered by a bathing suit!

KENNY. Do it and you'll starve.

EDITH. I'll make pizza. I can walk to the store. I have the other ATM card.

KENNY. Ed, get dressed right now.

EDITH. I don't have to do anything you say. You're not Dad!

KENNY. And it's a good thing, because Dad wouldn't take you to your recital or talk to you at all and you'd just be stuck here by yourself, all the time.

(**EDITH** *is fuming – she's about to explode.* **KENNY** *backs off. He starts to button his shirt, tuck it in, and so on.*)

KENNY. *(cont.)* You have to look nice for your recital. There will be pictures. You have your own solo. I'm trying to look nice. See? For you.

EDITH. You need me, too. Don't forget.

KENNY. I know.

EDITH. Without me, he'd leave you here all alone, too. Benji can't replace me.

KENNY. I don't want Benji to replace you.

EDITH. I'm wearing pants. The nice black ones, but pants. No dress.

KENNY. Okay. And brush your hair.

EDITH. I'll put it in a pony tail.

KENNY. Good.

(a beat)

EDITH. Does he even know about my recital?

KENNY. I'm sure he has a good reason for not coming.

EDITH. Like what?

KENNY. It isn't easy for him to get time off work.

EDITH. Max's dad came to Parent-Teacher conferences, and he's a doctor, too. Dad has to get time off. It's the law. He took time off before mom.

KENNY. Get changed.

EDITH. He doesn't deserve your loyalty.

KENNY. He's our father.

EDITH. Don't remind me. Remind him that we're his kids.

KENNY. He hasn't forgotten.

EDITH. DON'T DEFEND HIM.

KENNY. We're going to be late for your recital. We'll talk later.

EDITH. I'll be the only one without a parent there.

KENNY. Mom will be there. She's always there.

EDITH. She doesn't count, because she's not really there, is she?

KENNY. Yeah, she is, Eddie. How do you think we've made it this long? Mom's here. And when you sing your solo, she'll be so proud of you.

(**EDITH** *can't argue with that. She almost goes, but then...*)

EDITH. Can Benji come?

KENNY. You want...why do you...?

EDITH. Everyone will have a mom and a dad. So I'll have a you and a Benji. It'll be more fun.

KENNY. It'll be fun whether he goes or not. But...I'll ask him. If you want me to. If you want him to come. Do you want him to come?

EDITH. Whatever.

(**EDITH** *goes, at last.*)

(**KENNY** *looks at the phone. He's nervous. He plugs the phone back into the wall and dials. As the rotary dial click-click-clicks,* **BENJI** *enters.*)

(*The electronic ring of a phone.* **BENJI** *takes out a cordless and answers.*)

BENJI. I know it's you.

KENNY. Do you just say that every time you answer the phone?

BENJI. No, I know. The phone rings differently.

KENNY. Do birds suddenly appear?

BENJI. No. Stars light up in the sky.

KENNY. What are you doing tonight?

BENJI. An essay. Position paper.

KENNY. What position?

BENJI. Missionary. Con.

KENNY. Con?

BENJI. Pro doggy-style.

KENNY. It's all you ever think about, isn't it?

BENJI. And getting into a good school.

Hey, did you know that "boondocks" comes from a Filipino word?

KENNY. Okay...

BENJI. Like when you say someone lives in the boondocks. In the sticks. It's because bundok is the Filipino word for mountain and the mountains are in the middle of nowhere. American soldiers brought the word over.

KENNY. How do you – why do you know this?

BENJI. I was just reading some stuff. I thought it was cool. You're Filipino, and you live in the boondocks. And...

KENNY. Uh-huh.

BENJI. So...uh, what are you doing tonight?

KENNY. Ed has a thing. A recital. She wants to know if you want to go.

BENJI. She wants to know?

KENNY. Yeah. She said, "Is Benji going?"

BENJI. That's weird.

KENNY. Not really. Ed's weird.

BENJI. I know but...wait. Are you asking me out?

KENNY. WHAT? No, I'm not...Ed asked me if –

BENJI. Do you not want to ask me out?

KENNY. No, I just. It sounds weird: "Asking out."

BENJI. It's not any weirder than what we did under the bleachers yesterday.

KENNY. Come to the recital with us tonight.

BENJI. Us?

KENNY. Me.

BENJI. On a date.

KENNY. I...I guess. Really? A "date." Like, two guys on a date?

BENJI. All right. If it's too weird to take me to your sister's recital on a date, then I guess it's too weird for me to give you a handjob under the bleachers tomorrow.

(**KENNY** *pauses.*)

KENNY. You're like a prostitute.

BENJI. Shut up.

KENNY. You're a hooker.

BENJI. Bye.

KENNY. No, no, no, no. Wait. Okay.

BENJI. Date or handjob?

KENNY. Well, both. I mean, clearly I don't get one without the other. So I'm asking you on a date, to go with me to my sister's recital.

BENJI. Okay. I'd like that. To go on a date. But that doesn't mean I have to give you a handjob in exchange. If I do, it's because I want to. Not because I'm a hooker.

KENNY. Okay, whore. Whatever you need to tell yourself.

BENJI. Jerk.

KENNY. Bye, whore. I'll pick you up in twenty minutes, whore.

(KENNY *hangs up the phone.* BENJI *disappears.*)

(EDITH *enters, half-dressed.*)

EDITH. Did you ask him out?

KENNY. Did I...? Yes. We have to pick him up.

EDITH. Good. It's a date.

(EDITH *grins at him.*)

End of Scene

Space Is Infinite

(The front seat of a car, late at night. **KENNY** *drives* **BENJI** *home from* **EDITH***'s recital.)*

BENJI. Space is infinitely divisible. Say, for example, you have Point A and Point B, and they're ten centimeters apart, and you're going to bring them together by halves.

KENNY. Okay.

BENJI. So do it.

KENNY. So…five centimeters, two-point-five centimeters – or, I guess, twenty-five millimeters. One hundred twenty-five micrometers. Sixty-two-point-five micrometers?

BENJI. Or six hundred twenty-five nanometers.

KENNY. And on and on.

BENJI. Exactly: and on and on. Forever. When will you get to an order of magnitude, a unit of distance, of space that cannot be split?

KENNY. Theoretically, never.

BENJI. Because space is not particulate. There is no elementary particle for space. The distance by halves will never be completely traversed. A and B in theory will never come together, because space is infinite. Theoretically, moving by halves – by any fraction – nothing can touch. They can only connect if they go all the way. Isn't that mind-blowing? That's so cool. See? If you stayed awake in class, you'd know this stuff.

KENNY. Oh, my god. You're ridiculous.

BENJI. It is cool, though.

*(***KENNY*** pats ***BENJI***'s thigh.)*

KENNY. Okay, okay.

*(***KENNY*** leaves his hand where it is, and ***BENJI*** – let's face it – is 16 and in love for the first time, so…insta-boner.)*

BENJI. What are…what are you doing?

KENNY. You're such a nerd.

BENJI. No, I'm not.

KENNY. You've tried to seduce me with dictionary definitions, research about the Philippines, and theoretical calculus.

BENJI. Successfully, by the way.

KENNY. I'm not complaining. But don't kid yourself. You're in Band. You play clarinet.

(BENJI *lightly punches* KENNY's *shoulder.*)

Ow!

BENJI. I'm not a nerd.

KENNY. You hit me.

BENJI. Oh, sorry. Just testing the theory.

KENNY. Your theory is stupid.

(KENNY *reaches for* BENJI, *who tries to get away but is, of course, trapped by the car.* KENNY *pulls* BENJI's *head onto his shoulder and kisses it. He leaves his hand in* BENJI's *hair, stroking it gently.* BENJI *stops struggling.*)

You feel that?

BENJI. You didn't traverse the distance by halves. You went all the way.

KENNY. Is that okay?

BENJI. Yeah.

(BENJI *closes his eyes. They drive in silence.*)

KENNY. Huh.

BENJI. What?

KENNY. I told Edith that Mom would be watching her recital, and, in a way, I guess she really was there. Because if the distance between A and B and me and you and everything and everything else is infinitely divisible, then really my mom's only as far from me as you are now. Infinity.

BENJI. What happened to your mom?

KENNY. She left.

BENJI. I thought she died.

KENNY. She did. She loved us all very much. And if it were possible, she would have stayed with us forever. She never would have left any of us.

BENJI. You tell it like it's a story.

KENNY. It is. It's the first lie I ever told Edith. The biggest one.

BENJI. She's not dead?

KENNY. Of course she is. She…left. She…My mom and dad met in med school. Got married. Had us. And then Mom. She felt like my dad was not with her or us. Like he was distant, which he is. If you want proof that space cannot be traversed he's it, and eventually she got tired of it.

BENJI. And she just left.

KENNY. She cheated on him. With my fourth grade teacher.

BENJI. Whoa.

KENNY. And she moved away – Ed doesn't remember this. She was leaving him. She was going to get a place with Mr. Simons. Bill. And then when they were set up, she was going to come get us. But then, a month later, she got her diagnosis.

A brain tumor. And she knew it would be too confusing for Ed and me, both things at once. So she left Mr. Simons and came back to my dad. But only for us. And only to die. She left him. She came back. She left us all. And then he left Edith and me.

(**BENJI** *takes one of* **KENNY**'s *hands off the wheel and holds it close to him.* **KENNY** *is uncomfortable.*)

(**KENNY** *shrugs his shoulder and takes back his hand.* **BENJI** *sits up on his side of the car.*)

Now you think I'm some kind of freak. Some mopey… I'm not.

BENJI. Okay.

KENNY. And you can't tell Eddie.

BENJI. I won't.

KENNY. You can't tell anyone.

BENJI. Who have you told?

KENNY. No one.

BENJI. Why? You can't just deal with everything all by yourself.

KENNY. Except I do. Most of the time.

BENJI. You don't have to. I could…I don't know.

KENNY. You could what?

BENJI. I…don't know. I.

(**BENJI** *stares out the passenger side window.*)

(*silence*)

KENNY. Edith needs Mom to be perfect, you know? To think that she's always watching over her and caring for her. To know that mom didn't abandon her. Especially since my dad is…my dad.

BENJI. You're not a freak, Kenny. It's okay to miss your mom. If my mom were gone or left…I mean, I can't even imagine life without my mom.
And your mom didn't leave you. She was going to come get you. She loved you.

KENNY. Not enough to keep our family together. Edith needs to believe that our family is worth keeping together.

BENJI. She does or you do?

(*a beat*)

(**BENJI** *takes* **KENNY**'*s hand. This time,* **KENNY** *doesn't pull away.*)

KENNY. I ruined our date.

BENJI. No, you…you told me something you've never told anyone. This is the best date I've ever had.

KENNY. This is the only date you've ever had.

BENJI. Yeah, well, you, too.

(**KENNY** *turns the wheel, pulling into* **BENJI**'*s driveway.*)

KENNY. So…here we are.

BENJI. So.

KENNY. Okay, well. I guess…I'll see you tomorrow.

BENJI. Yeah. So…

(**KENNY** *leans in.* **BENJI** *looks panicked, and shrinks back.*)

KENNY. What? I…

BENJI. No, it's. I'm sorry.

KENNY. See? You don't. GOD – I shouldn't –

BENJI. NO. It's…my mom. She watches. Behind the curtain in the front window. She spies.

Last week, Stacy Stroud drove me home from practice, and when I went inside, my mom was like, "Why did Stacy take you home? Is she your girlfriend?" Not only did she see it was a she, she could see who it was.

I really want to kiss you, Kenny. Because of what you told me. But I can't.

(**KENNY** *turns away from him and stares out the window.*)

KENNY. She's watching.

BENJI. Yeah.

KENNY. Yeah.

BENJI. So I…Tell Edith I said she was great again.

KENNY. I will.

BENJI. First date. No kiss.

KENNY. It's fine.

BENJI. No, it's –

KENNY. I get it. Go. She's watching.

BENJI. Just…go?

KENNY. Go.

BENJI. Okay. I'll just. See you. Tomorrow.

KENNY. Okay. See you tomorrow.

(**KENNY** *continues to look away, unresponsive.*)

(**BENJI** *quietly opens the door. He steps out. He's barely holding it together.*)

(**BENJI** *shuts the door and runs off.* **KENNY** *puts the car in reverse and pulls away.*)

End of Scene

Faith

(**BENJI** *in his bedroom with his Pre-Calc text and bag. He listens to a Walkman while writing in his notebook. He sings quietly to himself as he does.*)

(**BENJI** *pushes his book aside and re-reads what he's written. He also continues to sing, a little bit louder now. He uses enough volume so that the words to* Faith *by George Michael can almost be heard.*)

BENJI. *(singing, full voice)*

BABY!

(**BENJI** *sings full voice as he tears the page out of his notebook and starts to fold it, origami-like, for easy passing in class.*)

(**BENJI** *finishes folding. Still singing, he takes the tape out of the Walkman and puts it together with the now folded note.*)

(**BENJI** *kisses the note and sings the chorus of the song to it one last time before he closes the note and tape into his book and stuffs them into his bookbag. When they're safely put away,* **BENJI** *suddenly breaks out his George-Michael-dancing-with-acoustic-air-guitar moves.*)

BENJI. *(cont'd)*

(singing and dancing)

DOO, DOO, DOO, DOO, DOO,
DOO, DOO, DOO, DOO, DOO,
DOO, DOO, DOO, DOO, DOO,
DUHN, D-DUHN, D-DUHN, D-DUHN DUHN...

(**BENJI** *dances offstage.*)

End of Scene

Budgeting Better

*(**KENNY** and **EDITH** in the living room. **KENNY** writes on a tablet. **EDITH** is playing with her bow throughout. The air rifle lies on the floor.)*

KENNY. Do you like school lunch?

EDITH. It's gross. The pizza is like paper and ketchup with dried glue on top, and the fries are raw inside. But I like on Friday when they get fish sandwiches from McDonald's. I like the tartar sauce.

KENNY. What if we made one big thing of food and kept that for lunch all week? Like mongo. Or a big pot of spaghetti.

EDITH. No, the baked kind.

KENNY. Ziti.

EDITH. Yeah! With the cheese on top. I like when you make that. And you know what I can make?

KENNY. What?

EDITH. Tuna salad. I was at Dina Osheyack's house and her mom made it, and it's SO EASY. You cut a celery into little squares, then an onion into littler squares, then you mix it with tuna, mayo, salt, and pepper, and lemon juice if you want. Then you make sandwiches.

KENNY. That's a great idea. So you're okay with packing lunches? It will save us money.

EDITH. Yeah, okay. Why do we need to save money?

KENNY. Same as before. In case he misses a week.

(pause)

EDITH. And…?

KENNY. Benji's dad is driving him over. He's going to stay with us. For a little while.

EDITH. How come?

KENNY. Because his mother is sick.

EDITH. I know when you're lying now.

KENNY. It's not a lie. She is a sick person.

(The doorbell rings.)

I'll be right back.

*(**KENNY** exits to answer the door. **EDITH** looks at the tablet he's left behind.)*

EDITH. I'll write a grocery list for my sandwiches. Tuna. Onion. Celery. Mayonnaise.

I know what else will save money.

Can you hear me?

It will be automatic, because if Benji stays here, you won't have to use any gas driving to his house.

*(**KENNY** enters with **BENJI**, holding his hand. **BENJI** looks the worse for wear. His clothes have been thrown on – perhaps his shirt buttons are one buttonhole off. His too long hair is unkempt. He has been or perhaps still is crying. His backpack is stuffed to overflowing with unfolded clothes.)*

EDITH. Is your mom that sick?

BENJI. What?

KENNY. Never mind.

EDITH. What happened to you?

KENNY. Ed. Back off. He's a guest.

EDITH. He's staying here now.

*(to **BENJI**)* You live here now, and you'll be safe, okay? Don't be scared.

*(**BENJI** sets down his backpack. **KENNY** sits on the couch and pats a spot for **BENJI** to sit. **BENJI** does. **EDITH** perches on the arm of the couch.)*

BENJI. I made a mixtape.

*(to **KENNY**)* For you. Some songs that made me think of you.

KENNY. Oh. Thanks.

BENJI. I put it in my schoolbag. And I wrote a note to give you with it. To pass to you in Pre-Calc tomorrow.

KENNY. And she found it.

BENJI. I'm doing my chores – washing dinner dishes. I go in my room when I'm done, and she's sitting there holding the tape and the note. Her face is all twisted. Disgusted. And then she yells for my dad and brother, and when they come in, she shoves the note at me and goes: "Read it. Aloud. To your father."

And I read. And she shakes and cries. And my brother swears. And my dad just stands there. I get to the end and I hear this...this crack sound. And she snapped it in half. Your tape.

(**BENJI** *goes to his bag and pulls out the ruined cassette and the note.*)

I snatched it from her. I don't know why. It's useless now. She tried to take the note, too, but I held onto it, because I had to give it to you.

And then things are so messed up. She tells my brother to take me outside. And he just picks me up and she yells and yells as he takes me out front and throws me out of the house. He actually threw me off the porch. And they go back in, and I don't know what to do, so I just sit there on the front lawn too scared to go back in. And I hear more yelling, until eventually my dad comes out with a bunch of my stuff. He puts me in the car and says he'll talk to her, and if that doesn't work maybe his sister can take care of me for a little while, but is there somewhere I can stay right now? I'm sorry I told him to call you. I don't mean to –

KENNY. Don't be sorry.

BENJI. My dad goes, "I'm going to make sure Mom talks to you tomorrow." But I don't want to talk to her. I don't want to go home, to...with her. I want her to leave me alone.

EDITH. Read the note.

BENJI. Huh?

EDITH. Just do it. Kenny's here now. Read it to him.

BENJI. I don't –

KENNY. It's okay, you don't. Ed…

EDITH. Just read it. It's right there. Just read it.

(**BENJI**, *still a bit stunned, starts to read the note.*)

BENJI. *(reading)*

"Dear Kenny, I don't know if you like all these songs, but they're mostly about not knowing how someone feels. So I really relate to them a lot, because sometimes I wonder what we're doing.

"If you relate, too, then I just want to tell you that you don't have to wonder about how I feel. You should have faith in me, and I hope hope hope that you want me to have faith in you.

"I can't dress stuff up with words like you do. Mostly, what I think or feel just comes out, so here it is. You make me feel really good. I'm happy when we're together. It's hard to concentrate on Pre-Calc homework, because you're in that class with me, and college and differential equations just can't compete. I hope you feel the same way. I have a feeling you do. Even if you don't, I hope you at least like the tape.

"Love, Benji."

(**BENJI** *lowers the note.*)

(*silence*)

(**KENNY** *stands up and kisses* **BENJI**.)

EDITH. See? Look what happened. Did anyone throw you out? Or cry? Or anything?

BENJI. No.

EDITH. You read the note, and you're going to stay right here. And Kenny's going to take care of you, like he takes care of me. And I'm going to make sure your mother doesn't come by here and talk to you until you want her to. I'm going to protect you.

(**EDITH** *puts the bow down and picks up the air rifle.*)

You're safe here. I'm going to secure the perimeter.

(**EDITH** *marches out the front door.* **KENNY** *picks up* **BENJI**'s *bag.*)

KENNY. We can put your stuff in my room. Come on.

(**BENJI** *doesn't move.* **KENNY** *holds out his hand.*)

Hey.

BENJI. Is it okay that I...what will your dad say?

KENNY. I...don't really care. Now, come on.

End of Scene

For Mother

(The next night. **EDITH** *drags her bucket into the living room along with her frog and air rifle. She keeps watch.)*

(She sings "Ein Männlein steht im Walde" to herself.)

EDITH. *(singing)*
Ein Männlein steht im Walde ganz still und stumm,
Es hat von lauter Purpur ein Mäntlein um.
Sagt, wer mag das Männlein sein,
Das da steht im Wald allein
Mit dem purpurroten Mäntelein.

Das Männlein steht im Walde auf einem Bein
Und hat auf seinem Haupte schwarz Käpplein klein,
Sagt, wer mag das Männlein sein,
Das da steht im Wald allein
Mit dem kleinen schwarzen Käppelein?

(She sits on the bucket.)

*(***BENJI** *enters from the bedroom, partly undressed, perhaps an undershirt and pants.)*

BENJI. Where's Kenny?

EDITH. Laundry room. Getting towels.

BENJI. What are you doing?

EDITH. Keeping watch.

BENJI. Is that your job?

EDITH. It's not a job. I just do it. Someone has to keep us safe. What are you doing?

BENJI. I just wanted to…may I have a glass of milk?

EDITH. You don't have to ask permission.

BENJI. My mom usually brings me milk, a glass of milk, when I'm not sleepy.

EDITH. So go get some milk.

*(***BENJI** *considers this and stands a moment uncertainly.)*

BENJI. I thought when I got up this morning or when we got back from school that your dad would be here. When is your dad going to be here?

EDITH. Doesn't matter. He wouldn't get you milk either. You need to take care of yourself.

BENJI. I know, but how do you know how to...to do that?

EDITH. I just do.

Sometimes I go to Dina Osheyack's house, and her mom is always there. She teaches us how to do stuff, helps us do our homework. And it's fun, even though Mrs. Osheyack can be really annoying. She wants to see Dina all the time and hear all about school and stuff.

But Mrs. Osheyack? She's always telling Dina what to do – pick this up and throw this out and show Tom some respect, he has cross country tomorrow! And, it's like, when she's around, Dina is actually dumber. Dina needs to be told what to do. Dina's mom wants her to be dumb, and Dina wants to be dumb for her mom. Well, I mean, Dina's a little dumb, anyway. But not that dumb.

And your mom? She wants to worry about you, to see and hear you, but only if you're dumb, too. Only if you do the things she wants to see and hear. So she kicked you out, and you're practically a baby. Do you want to be a baby forever?

BENJI. No.

EDITH. Right. You're almost as smart as me, and I don't need anyone. So just do what I do, and you'll be fine. Show her you're fine. Live here and be like me.

(*KENNY enters with some fresh dish towels, as* **EDITH** *positions herself, sniper-like, on the couch.*)

KENNY. I thought you were going to bed.

BENJI. I'm just going to get myself some milk.

KENNY. Oh, okay. I need to finish in the kitchen, and then I'll come to bed, too.

BENJI. I can help. At home, I usually do the dinner dishes.

KENNY. You don't have to.

BENJI. No, it'll be…it'll feel normal. It'll make me feel normal.

KENNY. It's nice to feel normal sometimes.

EDITH. SHHHHHHHHHH…

(EDITH raises a hand overhead, commandingly. They freeze. A tense moment, then she lowers her hand.)

As you were.

KENNY. Ed, don't stay up too late playing.

EDITH. I'm not playing.

KENNY. Whatever you're doing. What do you want for breakfast tomorrow?

EDITH. Fried rice.

BENJI. You eat fried rice for breakfast?

KENNY. Our mom used to make it.

(to EDITH)

Okay, fried rice. Not too late. You have to catch the bus tomorrow. I'm not driving you.

EDITH. Okay, okay.

(KENNY and BENJI head for the kitchen. BENJI lingers.)

BENJI. Thanks, Ed.

EDITH. For what?

(BENJI goes. EDITH keeps her sights trained on the door.)

(5 seconds.)

Fergie. I wish Mom was here.

(silence)

Now you sound like Kenny. I know she's here, like that. But I wish she was here here. Like, not dead. So she could protect us, instead of me.

(Lights change, indicating the passage of time.)

(Once again, EDITH has fallen asleep by the bucket.)

(The sound of a door opening slowly as a shaft of light expands over **EDITH**'s *prone body. Cutting across the light is the shadow of a person.)*

(The shadow is huge at first. It hesitates and then, with the accompanying sound of footsteps, it shrinks as the person casting it steps closer and closer to **EDITH**.)*

(Suddenly, **EDITH** *bolts up and grabs the gun. She aims it at the person casting the shadow, who backs up, causing the shadow to grow again.)*

EDITH. *(cont.)* HEY! WHO GOES THERE?

(The shadow stops.)

Just back away, lady. Just turn around and go right out the door. NOW.

(The shadow shrinks, coming closer.)

*(***EDITH** *pumps the rifle.)*

I said turn around. I'M NOT AFRAID TO USE THIS! I've got a bullet in here just for you…

(Pumps. The shadow freezes.)

I SAID GO AWAY. I – we're not defenseless. ARE YOU HIS MOM? Benji doesn't want to talk to you, okay?

(Pump pump pump! The shadow shrinks more.)

Go away.

GO AWAY!

I said…

*(***EDITH** *shoots. She hits.)*

(The person casting the shadow collapses.)

*(***BENJI** *enters from the bedroom in only a pair of briefs.)*

Go back in the room.

BENJI. What? Why?

EDITH. Just go…

*(***BENJI** *sees the shot person.)*

BENJI. Ed? What is – ? What…happened? What…?

EDITH. KENNY! KENNY!!!

(**KENNY** *enters, also in briefs, and sees the shot person.*)

KENNY. Ed! What did you do?

EDITH. I shot Benji's mom.

BENJI. What?

EDITH. I did. She wouldn't back away. I shot…And I shot. Her.

KENNY. Give me the rifle.

EDITH. NO!!!

BENJI. Kenny…

EDITH. I told her you didn't want to talk to her, but she just –

BENJI. That's not. I mean.

KENNY. Oh, my god.

BENJI. That's not my mom. That's not her. Not my mom.

EDITH. Then who did I shoot? Why is she here?

KENNY. Oh, my god. That's. That's Chloë, Edith. Remember from dinner? She and Dad – that's Chloë. That's Dad's –

EDITH. SHE WOULDN'T BACK AWAY. It's…her? It is?

(**KENNY** *stops as another shadow fills the shaft of light.*)

(**EDITH** *screams, startled.* **BENJI** *jumps for* **KENNY,** *half clutching him, half covering them both up.*)

(**KENNY** *pulls* **EDITH** *toward them. They all cower fearfully.*)

Daddy?

End of Scene

End of Act I

ACT II

Scared Robot

(**KENNY**, **EDITH**, *and* **BENJI** *sit at a round table in an ice cream parlor. They eat ice cream cups in silence – Rocky Road, Butter Pecan, and Strawberry Cheesecake respectively.*)

(*They look very, very tired.*)

EDITH. Can you have butter pecan ice cream without the ice cream?

KENNY. Yeah. They're called wet nuts.

EDITH. Wet nuts? That doesn't sound all that good.

BENJI. I love wet nuts.

KENNY. Even now, that's all you can think about.

BENJI. Especially now.

EDITH. What is?

KENNY. What is what?

EDITH. All he can think about.

BENJI. Wet nuts.

KENNY. Stop it.

BENJI. Even dry nuts would be nice.

EDITH. You mean dry roasted?

BENJI. Hey, Kenny, let's get our nuts.

(**KENNY** *slams down his ice cream and walks away, exiting the parlor.*)

(**EDITH** *and* **BENJI** *each eat a spoonful.*)

EDITH. I wouldn't have shot her if I knew who she was.

BENJI. He's mad at me, not you.

EDITH. He's mad at me, and you're standing in the way. If he stood up to things, I wouldn't have to. And then I wouldn't mess things up. If he had his way, we'd just be quiet and alone on that farm. Till we died. Surrounded by hay and grass and nothing.

BENJI. He's trying. To take care of you.

EDITH. I can take care of myself.

BENJI. Ed, you shot your future stepmother. She went to the hospital to get a pellet removed from her shoulder.

EDITH. She should have backed away. And she's basically a stranger. He should have called us and told us she was coming.

BENJI. He said he tried, but the phone was unplugged.

EDITH. And anyway I didn't mean it; I was protecting you.

BENJI. Except you didn't shoot – she wasn't even my –

EDITH. I thought I was protecting you, okay? You should be thankful. That's what I'd do for you. Kenny would just slither away, like he did just now.

BENJI. I don't really want you to shoot people for me. Not even my mom.

EDITH. Why? You want to shoot her yourself?

BENJI. No.

EDITH. What if she were going to shoot you?

BENJI. She would never do that. She's my mom.

EDITH. She's sitting at home right now with no idea whether you're eating, whether there's a roof over your head, whether you're even alive. You think someone capable of that could never shoot you, just because she gave birth to you?

BENJI. Stop it.

EDITH. Even if she loves you, her love doesn't mean anything. When it matters, it doesn't mean a thing.

(**KENNY** *re-enters.* **EDITH** *and* **BENJI** *clam up.* **KENNY** *walks deliberately to the table and sits. Without a word, he starts eating his ice cream again.*)

(**EDITH** *stares angrily at* **BENJI** *as she rapidly shovels the rest of her ice cream into her mouth. When she finishes, she turns to* **KENNY**.)

EDITH. *(cont.)* I'm cold. I left my coat in the car.

(**KENNY** *hands her the keys.* **EDITH** *exits.*)

BENJI. I'm sorry. I was trying to make you laugh.

KENNY. No, it's…I'm sorry. It's hard to laugh right now.

BENJI. Okay, so what should we do next?

KENNY. I don't know. I wasn't thinking. She shot Chloë and I switched into automatic. I thought, while he brings Chloë to the hospital, get Edith in the car and out of there as fast as possible. But that…that was all. It's just…the way he screamed at her. And the way she screamed back. And the rifle, still in her hands. I was like, "She's going to shoot him. Ed'll shoot him, too." Which is ridiculous.

BENJI. I can see why you would have thought that.

KENNY. But now, we've been sleeping in the car for two days, we can't keep skipping school, and we only have money for a week, at most. And I don't…it's like I got us in even deeper trouble than we were. I'm such a. GOD – WHAT A FUCKING LOSER. I'm such a fucking idiot.

BENJI. You're not an –

KENNY. We don't have anywhere to live. I don't make any money. I can't take care of us. Of her. I don't know how. I look like I've got it together, but Ed's right: I'm a robot who learned a program. If this, then that. But I'm not programmed for this. We're trapped in that house, and now that I got us out, I don't know what to do or where to go.

(a beat)

BENJI. You know the first thing Ed said to me?

KENNY. What?

BENJI. She walked right up to me and went, "I can shoot things. I can hit stuff."

KENNY. Well, she wasn't lying.

BENJI. Totally. I could never shoot someone.

KENNY. I'm glad. I don't want you to shoot anyone.

BENJI. And, like, when you're planning what groceries to get so you can make dinner and lunch and all the food for the week? I can't do that. I couldn't take Ed to school and extra-curriculars and still get straight A's in Pre-Calc and Chem.

KENNY. I got a B in Chem.

BENJI. I couldn't do half the stuff you can do. My mom tells me what to wear, and when kids used to be, like, "Your mom dresses you. Loser!" I didn't know why that was an insult, because I didn't really know that other people could do stuff. The only food I can make is a bowl of cereal. I still have my learner's permit. My mom does everything for me. Did.

KENNY. Do you miss her?

BENJI. No. Not...not really.

KENNY. Then why are you telling me this?

BENJI. Because you're not a loser.

You and Edith. You're all alone in that house and sometimes it's creepy and sometimes you're running out of money, but you can take care of yourselves. I would just be helpless. Or scared.

KENNY. But I am. I'm really scared, Benji. What have I gotten us into? Fine. Edith can shoot things and hit them. But she shouldn't have to shoot things. And I'm not a robot. I should be allowed to be scared sometimes instead of always fixing things. I just want to sit and be scared and for things to be okay.

(*BENJI brushes his fingers against* **KENNY**'s *hand.*)

BENJI. Okay.

(*BENJI slips his hand under the table.* **KENNY** *does, too, so they can hold hands.*)

KENNY. What if people see?

BENJI. The only person I care about now is you. So don't look at anyone but me. Just be scared for a minute. Okay? Be scared. And then we'll figure out what to do. And I'll help. I can help. You won't have to do it by yourself.

KENNY. Okay.

(10 seconds.)

*(***KENNY*** *really does look terrified.* ***BENJI*** *squeezes his hand, and after a moment the fear starts to fade.)*
SHE SHOT HER.

(They both start to laugh, uncontrollably.)

BENJI. Edith shot your stepmother.

KENNY. Potential stepmother. Or, I mean, formerly potential stepmother. I can't imagine she'll want anything to do with us now.

BENJI. Why, because she walked into the house and got shot in the shoulder with a BB?

KENNY. And the part where she walked in on my boyfriend and I in our undies.

BENJI. Maybe that'll be a plus in the whole, "Should I be a step-mother?" debate. Con: step-daughter with air rifle. Pro: step-son who looks good in undies.

KENNY. That's just...EW.

(a beat)

I should take you home.

BENJI. What?

KENNY. To your dad. You should go home, Benji. It's our mess.

BENJI. I don't want to. I'm going to help. You'll see.

*(***EDITH*** *enters, wearing her coat, looking utterly defeated. She's been crying.)*

EDITH. He's standing at the car.

He says you have one chance to walk out on your own, bring me with you, and drive back home.

He says if you don't, he'll tell the police that you kidnapped me and stole the car. He said Benji's mom wants to tell the police that we kidnapped Benji.

(silence)

KENNY. We're trapped.

*(**KENNY** stands up.)*

EDITH. Don't do it, Kenny, please. Let's sneak out the back or something. Don't.

*(**KENNY** heads for the door.)*

Don't, Kenny. PLEASE. PLEASE!!!

KENNY. We're going back. If the police get involved and catch us, they could take you away from me.

EDITH. They won't catch us. Let's run. Let's fly away.

KENNY. Edith, we're kids. We're just kids.

*(**KENNY** takes **EDITH**'s hand. **EDITH** reaches out to **BENJI**, who takes her other hand.)*

(All three look petrified as they exit the ice cream parlor.)

End of Scene

Uniform

(**EDITH** *stands in the living room.* **KENNY** *enters with a girl's school uniform, which he helps her into. It's like a Catholic School uniform, but even more drab, sexless, and depressing.*)

EDITH. Where is he?

KENNY. He'll be here tomorrow morning to drive you to the school. Are you packed?

EDITH. Yes. What about you?

KENNY. He wants me to stay here. Or, I mean, at my school. Now you get to leave, but I'm stuck here.

EDITH. I hate him, Kenny.

KENNY. Don't say that, Ed. You can't hate him.

EDITH. He's splitting us up.

KENNY. He can't split us up.

EDITH. He is.

(**EDITH** *is now dressed. She looks ridiculous, like a wild animal on a leash.*)

KENNY. It looks...all right.

EDITH. It looks stupid.

KENNY. It looks stupid.

EDITH. Let's get out of here. We'll get in the car, but we'll do it right this time. We'll drive and drive and drive until we never have to see him again.

KENNY. I'm going to tell you a story.

EDITH. I don't want any more of your stupid stories.

KENNY. It's mom's story. She told it to us when we were little. You're too young to remember.

There's this turtle and this monkey, who is always trying to trick the turtle but never quite manages to, because he's too clever and patient. Like this one day, they fight over who gets to keep a banana plant they found. The monkey threatens to take the whole tree, but the turtle says, "Let's split it in half. Pick the half you want." So the monkey chops off the top of the tree, runs home, eats all the bananas, and thinks, "That stupid turtle. Hungry and sitting in the sun."

KENNY. *(cont.)* But the next time the monkey sees the turtle, he's napping under a beautiful banana plant with lots of fruit and foliage, because the turtle was clever.

EDITH. He kept the bottom of the tree and planted it.

KENNY. And patiently waited for it to grow. Right. So, envious of the new tree, the monkey scrambles up its trunk and eats all of the turtle's bananas and then falls asleep.

Finally, the turtle decides to teach him a lesson. He surrounds the tree with thorny branches and yells, "Crocodile! Crocodile!" until the startled monkey bolts awake, runs down, and gets stuck with thorns. In a fury, the monkey snatches up the turtle and says, "For that, I'm going to kill you!"

"Please don't!" says the turtle.

EDITH. I don't like this monkey.

KENNY. "I could smash you on the rocks or rake you over hot coals! Or I could drown you in the ocean!" The turtle knows he's too slow to run away, so he begs, "Don't drown me! Smash me or throw me in the coals – just don't drown me!"

And with that, the monkey bolts for the ocean, tosses the turtle in, and sits back to laugh as he drowns. But, of course –

EDITH. The turtle swims away.

KENNY. Because he's a slow turtle, too little to break free. But he's clever and patient, so he just waits for the monkey to set him free. You see?

EDITH. Yeah. Better than you do.

Mom is dead, Kenny. You can't just pull her out when you want me to feel better.

KENNY. I'm not. I don't do that.

EDITH. Yes, you do! When I won't do what you say, you make it what she says to get your way. She's not one of your lies. She's our mom. And she can't help us anymore.

KENNY. She is helping us. And this time you better let me get my way.

Dad could do a lot worse than this school, and he still might. You shot someone. You could be locked up in juvie or drugged up in some hospital for crazy kids. We can't let this get any worse.

So you do what I tell you and lay low. Go to this school. They'll try to tell you what to do: what to wear, how to eat, when to get up, and when to go to bed. Let them. Hide. Be patient, like the turtle. Just be a little bit like me.

EDITH. Clever. And patient. Maybe you have to be a little bit like me. To stop him. You cannot let him kick me out of this house.

KENNY. He's dad.

EDITH. If you don't do something, I will.

KENNY. No. The things you do have consequences.

EDITH. The things you don't do have consequences, too.

KENNY. We didn't get into this mess because of something I didn't do. Wait until I figure this out, or he comes to his senses.

EDITH. WHAT? He's not going to just wake up and say, "I made a big mistake!"

KENNY. We don't know that.

EDITH. You're glad he's getting rid of me.

KENNY. SHUT UP.

EDITH. You leave all the time. To go to Benji's. To get away when he comes home. You don't want me here. You're just like him.

KENNY. I am your brother, and I love you.

EDITH. SO HELP ME. Help me or you're going to be stuck here by yourself all the time and –

KENNY. How am I supposed to help you, when I can't even help myself? I'm sixteen, Ed! And he's dad. I can't fight him. I can't keep you out of trouble or stay awake in class or stop Benji's mom. I can't even make you catch the bus. I can't!

EDITH. I catch the bus. Most of the time.

I wish Mom was here to tell us stories or to teach us how to make tuna fish sandwiches or to worry about me staying out too late. Or sometimes I wish dad would do those things. But they won't. They're not here.

You are. And I am. And one of us has to stop him.

(**KENNY** *is silent, helpless before her.*)

Forget it. I don't need you.

KENNY. Eddie.

EDITH. Let him send me to that school, and I'll get out before you know it. That's how clever I'll be.

End of Scene

Fixing It

*(The living room a week later. **KENNY** does Pre-Calc homework. The cordless phone is nearby.)*

(There's no sound other than his pencil on paper.)

*(**KENNY** stops and looks around as if there should be someone there, but there isn't. No one is there.)*

(Time passes. He's completely alone.)

*(He takes something out from under the front cover of his textbook. A worn piece of paper, **BENJI**'s note.)*

KENNY. *(singing)*

Well, I guess it would be nice,
If I could touch your body.

*(**KENNY** sets the book aside and dials the phone.)*

(into the phone)

Hi. Is Benji there? I mean, Ben. It's Kenny.
Oh.
Okay. He can call back after dinner, I'll be home.
Oh.
Okay. Thanks, Mrs. –

*(**KENNY** is hung up on before he can finish. He leans back on the couch and starts to read the note.)*

(Suddenly, the TV flips on.)

TV.

Is that a gnome here? Or that a gnome there?
And when we find her will she care...

*(**KENNY** sits up, stuffs his hands between the cushions, and pulls out the remote control and the scrambled Rubik's Cube. He flips off the TV.)*

(a beat)

*(**KENNY** picks up the phone again. Dials.)*

KENNY. *(into the phone)* Hi. Ed Tolen – Edith Tolentino, please.

Her brother. Kenny.

Oh. When can she receive phone calls?

Okay. Thanks.

(KENNY hangs up and looks at the Rubik's Cube.)

Fix it.

(With several deft moves, KENNY solves the Cube.)

(He stares into space. He stares. And stares. And stares.)

End of Scene

Making Passes

(The sound of a school bell ringing.)

*(**KENNY** and **BENJI** on opposite sides of the stage. **BENJI** pulls out a note folded like a football. As he opens it and starts to read, **KENNY** speaks its contents aloud.)*

KENNY. Benji – Since when does Tom Osheyack care if we're hanging out? I can only surmise that Tom has a deep, unrequited (question mark) crush on you. The sight of me talking to you fills his spleen with jealous bile that courses through his veins and drips out of his every pore.

Meet me in the parking lot after school, and I'll give you a ride. I'll drive you home, too. – Kenny

(School bell. They take a step closer to each other.)

*(**KENNY** pulls out a note folded like a ninja star. As he opens it and starts to read, **BENJI** speaks its contents aloud.)*

BENJI. Ken – My brother is on wrestling and cross country with Tom. My mom doesn't want me talking to you, and he told his friends to help keep us separated. I was home when you called last night, too, but she wouldn't let me have the phone.

Believe me, the only thing boner-inducing about Tom Doucheyack is the idea of you punching him, so his love will have to stay unrequited.

Also, my brother is driving me home. We're going to have to be even sneakier than usual. – Ben

*(School bell. Step. **BENJI** reads the note in his hands; **KENNY** speaks its contents.)*

KENNY. B – Your mom sucks. And I refuse to believe that you and your brother are actually related. Although it's kind of sexy all this sneaking around, don't you think? – K

*(School bell. Step. **KENNY** reads; **BENJI** speaks.)*

BENJI. Ken doll – Not as sexy as me doing this to you.

(**BENJI** *draws a lewd picture in the air.* **KENNY**'s *eyes bug out of his head.*)

As you can surmise, I need to see you and not just in Pre-Calc. What do we do? – Big Ben

(*School bell. Step.* **BENJI** *reads;* **KENNY** *speaks.*)

KENNY. Benjamin – We can meet up 6th period away from prying eyes. Ask Ms. Olds if you can spend study hall doing research in the library. She'll let you – you're too sweet to be untrustworthy. I'll get out of Comp by saying that I want to go to guidance. With everything that happened to Edith, there's no way Ms. Seaver will say no. I'll meet you in the library by the science books. Biology. Barely anyone goes to that back table. No one will keep us apart. They can try all they want. But Edith's gone, and you're all I've got. She's really gone – Kenneth

(*School bell. Step. They now stand next to each other.*)

(*Pre-Calc. They stow their notes and then* **BENJI** *pulls out a new note folded into a heart. They hold their arms out,* **BENJI** *drops the note, and it lands in* **KENNY**'s *hand.*)

(**KENNY** *reads;* **BENJI** *speaks.*)

BENJI. Kenny – Good plan. I don't know how you come up with this stuff. Have you ever lied to me?

(**KENNY** *looks up at* **BENJI**.)

And they are keeping us apart, aren't they? Why? We aren't hurting anyone.

See you in the library. I will now spend the rest of Pre-Calc trying not to look like I'm gazing longingly at you. – Benji

(**KENNY** *stows the heart note, writes in his notebook, and turns it to* **BENJI**.)

(**BENJI** *reads;* **KENNY** *speaks.*)

KENNY. I have never lied to you. I never will. Can't wait for the library. I'm going to gaze longingly at you right now.

(**BENJI** *looks up at* **KENNY.**)

End of Scene

Going Solo

(**EDITH** *in a schoolyard. She's dressed to leave and talking to the frog.*)

EDITH. Okay, Fergie. This is probably our biggest mission ever, and it's not that I think you can't handle it…But we have to execute every stage with utmost precision, or it's over before it even starts. It's just me and you now. You're all I have.

You.

A stuffed frog.

From my mom. My mommy.

Let's review the mission parameters. To blow this joint, what we have to do is – I mean, what you have to do. I don't know what you have to do. What I have to do is…

Stop talking to a stupid stuffed frog who never really did anything.

Maybe, Fergie, it's time for me to go it alone. I don't think mom really gave you to me anymore, and that when I talk to you I'm talking to her. I'm not talking to anyone.

Because Kenny is a liar. He lies, and it's not funny anymore. He tells stories, like that mom got us all Christmas presents before she died. And that dad asks about me when he calls. And that he's going to come and get me. Because Kenny's not going to come and get me. The only person who can take care of me is me. I've got to do this all by myself, like I have to do everything. No Kenny, no mom, and no you. I'm going solo.

I don't need you, frog.

(**EDITH** *puts the frog on the ground and turns away.*)

(*10 seconds.*)

(**EDITH** *turns back to the frog, snatches her up and holds her at arms length.*)

EDITH. *(cont.)* It's just…I. I'm alone now, Fergie. And I had to. It was a test. Because what we're doing is dangerous and important and probably illegal. So I had to know I could trust you. Because it's hard to know who to trust now that we're all alone.

Because this…this is the test. THE test. Kenny can't come, because I have to prove to him that I'm a grown up. That it's time to grow my wings and fly away.

Fergie, we have to get rid of any parts of us that are still little girls. No more useless, weak, little girls. I'm going to take care of everyone. You. Kenny. Even Benji.

But first we have to make sure that he's taken care of. Permanently. Make sure he can never leave us in a place like this again. Never, ever again. So I had to be sure that we were in this together no matter what.

(EDITH takes some matches out of her pocket, strikes one, and watches it burn.)

Here we go.

End of Scene

Curly Fries

(**KENNY** *and* **BENJI** *sitting at a table in the school library.* **KENNY** *has a few books.* **BENJI** *has his usual gigantic, overstuffed backpack.*)

KENNY. Come over.

BENJI. I'm not supposed to.

KENNY. I liked it better when she'd given up on you.

BENJI. Me, too. At least we were getting laid.

Dad says it's not punishment; I'm just not allowed to leave because we all need to spend more time together. But when he goes to work, Mom barely speaks to me, because to her it IS punishment. And my stupid brother is just a dick. He tries to push or kick or hit me, and then he says something lame to piss me off like, "Fag!" or, "Pussy!" or, "Jesus saves!" And she lets him. So I tell him to quit touching me or he'll get my gay cooties. And then he walks around like some big stud being all, "I'm not queer. I screwed Jemma Lieber." And I actually think, as of two days ago, he is screwing Jemma. But my mom won't say a word, because it comforts her. Like her oldest son is more of a man because he's boning a brainless perpetual shopping machine.

KENNY. God.

BENJI. So then I go, "You know what makes you a man? Taking it up the butt – if you can do that, you can do ANYTHING."

KENNY. WHAT?!

BENJI. Yeah. And then my brother punched me in the gut. And my mom locked me in my room. My mom will never let me go to your house again.

(**BENJI** *takes the sleeve of* **KENNY**'*s shirt between his fingers, trying to look casual.*)

But we'll always have Pre-Calc.

KENNY. So romantic.

BENJI. And maybe...my dad. He's taking me to dinner on Thursday. Just me and him. To A&W. I like the curly fries.

Do you want to come?

KENNY. With your dad?

BENJI. Yeah. He...wants to meet you. "He's your boyfriend. Shouldn't I meet your boyfriend?"

KENNY. Are you serious?

BENJI. You called me your boyfriend. When we got ice cream. I didn't – you said it, and I...

KENNY. Oh.

BENJI. I shouldn't have taken it so seriously. You were freaking out, but I...

KENNY. Okay.

BENJI. Yeah?

KENNY. Thursday. A&W. Will you pick me up, or should I drive?

BENJI. We'll pick you up. And he'll probably pay for everything, so...

KENNY. So...another date.

BENJI. Yeah. Sort of. With a chaperone.

What did your dad say? He saw us that night, so he knows.

KENNY. Yeah. He asked who you were. I told him. And he just...stared at me. Blankly. Like he...

he didn't care.

BENJI. He's such a jerk.

KENNY. He's my dad.

BENJI. Can't you just say he's a jerk? Why do you defend him?

KENNY. Now you sound like Ed. Whatever. I don't care what he thinks. It's better if he doesn't care. If he leaves us alone.

BENJI. Your dad doesn't care enough. My mom cares too much.

KENNY. Yeah, right? Anyway, what's important now is Ed. I need to get her out of there, but I don't know how.

    I used to leave her alone, Benji. And now I'm there alone, and it's so quiet. Edith used to watch the same stupid movies over and over again – like this gnome musical thing. And I never knew why. But now I know. Without her there's nothing there.

    But what can I tell my dad so he'll take Edith out of that school? Nothing I come up with seems good enough to do the job.

BENJI. That's your answer. There's nothing to come up with. There's no story to tell.

KENNY. I can't just leave her there.

BENJI. Don't. Tell him that he can't leave her, because... he can't. You need to help your sister. And you need to stop telling stories to pretend your dad's not a jerk or to avoid confronting people or just to get your way.

KENNY. No, I have to at least...I can't stop –

BENJI. Kenny, if you don't, then you will one day, eventually, lie to me.

KENNY. No, I won't.

    (pause)

    I won't!

BENJI. Tell him the truth, Kenny.

KENNY. I...I don't know how to do that.

BENJI. You'll figure it out. You take it up the butt, remember? You can do anything.

    (BENJI tugs at KENNY's shirt again.)

KENNY. I think about how you smell. Is that weird?

BENJI. How do I smell?

KENNY. Like Ivory soap. And dryer sheets.

BENJI. I think about your hand on the back of my head. Your fingers in my hair.

    I really want to kiss you, Kenny.

KENNY. Your brother might see. He'll tell your mom.

BENJI. She can't treat me any worse than she's already treating me.

KENNY. Benji, let's at least – we'll go somewhere, or –

(**BENJI** *kisses* **KENNY.**)

BENJI. I don't want us to hide. I don't want you to hide. Tell him the truth. They threw us out, or threw us away. They have no right anymore to tell us what to do.

End of Scene

Wild and Free

(**KENNY** *and the phone. He reconnects it to the wall.*)

(*It starts to ring immediately. Surprised,* **KENNY** *waits a moment and then answers.*)

KENNY. Eddie?

Oh. Hi. I was just about to call you. We need to – NO. Wait!

(*Yelling from the phone.* **KENNY** *takes it away from his ear, steels himself, and then brings the phone back in.*)

LISTEN TO ME. IF YOU WON'T TELL US WHAT TO DO SO THINGS GO RIGHT, THEN YOU CANNOT TELL US WHAT TO DO WHEN THINGS GO WRONG.

You have to take Edith out of that whatever you've sent her to. I mean, reform school? She has perfect grades, she sings choir. She has good friends.

You put me in charge, so I'm in charge. Understand? You aren't a parent. You're an interruption. I take care of this house and of Edith, so I decide whether she lives here and how. So before this goes too far, bring her back here or you will never see her again.

That's not a threat.

You made us. You raised us to need nothing except the money in the bank. We used to want you to come back. But now when you're here all we want is for you to leave. I took what you left us and made a home. Our home. We don't need your supervision or your new girlfriend or your decisions about reform school. I can get us everything we need. Without you. You left us wild and free. You can't cage us now.

So if you don't want to lose us forever, call that school and bring Edith home. Now. She doesn't need to be reformed. She's Edith. And she's twelve years old. She needs to come back to her home.

(**KENNY** *listens.*)

KENNY. *(cont.)* What?

That school is supposed to be a prison.

*(**KENNY** listens.)*

Wait.

Don't worry. I'll find her. You don't even know where to look.

*(**KENNY** hangs up the phone.)*

End of Scene

Fly High as the Sky

*(The barn. **KENNY** stands next to the haystack at the foot of the rafter and its support. In his hand is a plate with a tuna salad sandwich on it.)*

KENNY. How long have you been here?

*(The sound of a match being struck. A lit match flies from behind the rafter onto the floor of the barn. **KENNY** stomps it out.)*

Eddie.

*(**EDITH** appears from behind the cross support. She perches on the rafter.)*

EDITH. Is he home?

KENNY. No.

*(**EDITH** lights a match and throws it to the ground. **KENNY** stomps it out.)*

Stop it.

EDITH. That school was like a prison, except no one did anything cool like rob someone or kill someone or something. They just beat up a third grader or flashed their panties at the wrong person. And the other girls there are retarded. Does he think I'm retarded?

KENNY. Of course not. And you shouldn't say that. They're troubled.

EDITH. I'd be troubled, too, if I was retarded. Some of them can't even read or spell. They're the same age as me, but they can't. And some of them just stare like zombies, until you tell them what to do, and then they do as they're told. And the other ones are big, brutish, ogre girls. They're loud and stand up for themselves, but they're too dumb to know what they're standing up for. I can do fractions and decimals and negative numbers. I learned all that German for my choir solo. I can shoot an aluminum can from fifty feet away.

Is that what he thinks I am: troubled?

KENNY. You shot Chloë.

EDITH. I tried your way the first couple of days. And it worked: they trusted me. But I couldn't take those other girls and all the adults kept telling me what to do. They were easy to trick, because they're used to matching wits with those troubled girls. Not with me.

One girl was there for setting stuff on fire. She hid all these boxes of matches in her rolled up socks. So I stole a box and, before she could see any were missing, I reported her to the teachers. The next day, I packed a bag and set the trash behind the kitchen on fire. They went after the other girl, and I walked right out of there.

KENNY. How'd you get home?

EDITH. I hitchhiked to the bus station. Then I used the other ATM card to get money, buy a ticket, and pay Dina Osheyack's brother so he would pick me up at the station.

Is he here? Did they call him?

KENNY. Yes. But he doesn't know you're here.

EDITH. Where else would I go? I don't know how to go anywhere else. But you know what I realized? I shouldn't have to.

KENNY. You want to see him?

EDITH. I hate him. I'm going to surprise him. This is our house, Kenny. He can't kick me out. He's never here. I'm going to kick him out.

KENNY. That will definitely be a surprise.

(**EDITH** *starts to light another match.*)

(*stopping her*)

Ed, I have a sandwich for you. I made tuna salad this morning.

EDITH. You did?

KENNY. Yeah. Your recipe. I wanted to get it right for when you came back. You want it?

EDITH. When he gets home, I'm going to set his room on fire. And if he won't leave, then you and me can just get in the car and fly on out of here.

KENNY. I don't think that's what you really want, Ed.

EDITH. Sure it is. I'm not going back there.

KENNY. You don't have to. I told you to wait till I took care of everything, and I have.

EDITH. Liar.

KENNY. You can tell when I'm lying, right? So listen to me now: I told him I won't let him do this to you. To us. You're not going anywhere and you don't have to run away, okay?

Now just get down, eat this sandwich, come into the house, and then watch some TV while I make dinner.

EDITH. He sent me to that place. That's what he thinks I am. That's probably what he thinks you are. That's why he never comes here.

Three hours in that car with him, the most time we've been together in years, and then he just leaves me there. Drops me off, like he's taking out the trash.

(**EDITH** *stands on the rafter.*)

He'll never do that to me again. I'm a big girl. I am out of his reach. I am free as a bird. I am high as the sky!

KENNY. Ed, come down.

EDITH. He thinks we're troubled.

KENNY. Please.

EDITH. Retarded.

KENNY. Please, Ed.

EDITH. Worthless. We're nothing to him.

KENNY. We're everything to him, and he can't stand it.

(*a beat*)

You look like her. And now, you've started sounding like her. That's why he can't talk to you. Or see you. Us. You look like her, and I act like her. Dressing you up, fried rice for breakfast, telling her stories. In some ways I am her.

EDITH. But she's dead.

KENNY. Yeah.

EDITH. Does he want us to die, too?

KENNY. I don't know.

EDITH. That's not an excuse, Kenny. He's the grown up.

KENNY. I'm just explaining.

EDITH. He's abandoned us. And if you keep defending him, then, in some part of you, you think he's right to just leave us here. Is he right?

KENNY. No.

EDITH. Are you sure?

KENNY. Yes.

EDITH. Are. You. Sure?

KENNY. Yes, Edith. He's a jerk, okay? A jerk. He's a jerk, and I hate him. I hate him, too. And that's the truth. But you can't keep this up. You're going to hurt yourself.

EDITH. I told you. I'm going to fly out of here. Fly high as the sky. I'm going to take care of everything. I'll get us all out of here.

KENNY. But Benji and I need to stay here. And we both need you. To stay with us. Dad may not need you, but we do. You were gone, and then he told me you were missing, and I was so worried. What would I do without you? I need you.

EDITH. But I can't keep you safe.

KENNY. You don't have to. Don't be a big girl yet. Just come down, eat this sandwich, play with Fergie, and watch TV with me. That's all I need you to do.

We don't need you to protect us anymore. You just have to be a little girl. Be a little girl for me for a little while longer.

EDITH. You need me. To be a little girl?

KENNY. Yeah. I'll be the big one now. I promise. One that you can count on. Now come down. Don't fly away from me. Please. Please, just come on down.

(**EDITH**, *still standing on the rafter, starts to cry.*)

EDITH. I'm really hungry, Kenny.

KENNY. I know.

EDITH. I've been waiting up here for so long. For him to come back. But he never comes back. I just wait and wait and wait.

KENNY. So stop waiting. We don't...we don't need him. This is all you need right now: a sandwich. Okay?

EDITH. Okay.

(**EDITH** *balls up her hands into fists and wipes away her tears. She crouches down on the rafter, shaking with emotion. As she puts her hands down on the wood...*)

(*She loses her footing. Her hands, wet with tears, slip.* **EDITH** *falls behind the haystack.*)

(*THUD*)

(**KENNY** *gasps.*)

(*silence*)

KENNY. ...Edith?

(**KENNY** *drops the plate and sandwich.*)

EDITH?!

(*He runs behind the haystack.*)

(*The sound of a siren, which gets louder and louder.*)

End of Scene

Homecoming

(BENJI in the living room. KENNY sits on the couch listening to him with the cordless phone in his lap.)

BENJI. So I'm just there with my mom. And she has the phone in her hand. And she threatens me. She actually says she'll kill me. Or if I call you, it will kill her. And all I'm thinking is, "Edith escaped. She stole matches, lied to the authorities, committed arson, went AWOL, hitchhiked, stole money from your dad's bank account, hopped on a bus, bribed Tom Osheyack, and hid in the barn for a whole day before anyone found her."

Edith is twelve years old.

I'm sixteen, and all I want to do is call my boyfriend. And so I hold out my hand and say, "Give. Me. The phone."

And my mom hangs onto it with this fierce, angry terror. So I just snatch it from her, and I wait for her to scream or to hit me or to turn hysterical. But instead she just stands there like she's hiding in the corner. She's right in the middle of the room, but her face is like she's hiding in the corner.

And I call you. And we talk. And then I tell her I'm going to your place and don't wait up, because I'm spending the night.

Because Edith tried to fly, you know? And I thought, "She tried." And maybe she didn't make it, but she tried.

KENNY. I can't believe you talked to her like that.

BENJI. Me, either.

KENNY. Or that she went along with it.

BENJI. I've never actually stood up to her. It caught her off guard.

But she's been kind of leaving me alone, and I like it. I like picking my clothes. I'm going to pick my classes next semester. I'm going to take Art. And I made scrambled eggs for myself, and she was shocked. She was like, "How did you learn to do that?"

KENNY. And you said, "My boyfriend taught me," like a silly little girl.

BENJI. You're a girl.

KENNY. You wouldn't be here if I was a girl.

BENJI. Maybe I would. And you'd be pregnant like Jemma Lieber.

KENNY. Your brother's an idiot.

BENJI. So's my mom. She wanted a studly, super hetero son, and she got one. And now she'll be a grandma before the age of forty. Or stud son will have caused an abortion – I don't know which is worse to her. I was all, "Be careful what you wish for," and, "At least I can guarantee that Kenny'll never get pregnant."

My problems are nothing ever since Jemma's love-child. My dad was all, "Ben is getting good grades. He takes care of himself. He would never do anything as irresponsible as this. Back off of him. And this Kenneth is a stand-up fellow."

KENNY. I'm a what? "Kenneth?"

BENJI. Yeah, I think my dad has a crush on you or some-thing.

KENNY. You're sick.

BENJI. You're a stand-up fellow.

(The sound of the oven timer going off in the kitchen. **KENNY** *starts to get up.)*

No, I'll get it.

KENNY. Come on, don't –

BENJI. No, I will. I just have to put the potatoes in, right?

KENNY. And then stir.

BENJI. Potatoes and stir. I can do it. Just…sit.

*(***KENNY** *does.* **BENJI** *smiles and then exits.)*

*(***KENNY** *grabs the phone and wills it to ring. Nothing happens. He checks his watch and then sighs, heavily.)*

*(***BENJI** *re-enters, wearing oven mitts.)*

Maybe we should do homework or something.

KENNY. I can't – couldn't concentrate.

BENJI. Just to occupy yourself. You should occupy yourself.

KENNY. It's so late.

BENJI. There would have been a call if something happened.

KENNY. God, I can't believe she –

BENJI. Hey.

(*BENJI sits next to him on the couch. He takes* **KENNY***'s head into his oven mitt hands and kisses him.*)

KENNY. What are you doing?

BENJI. Distracting you.

KENNY. What are the mitts for?

BENJI. I put the potatoes in the pot like you said.

KENNY. With the mitts on?

BENJI. The lid was hot.

KENNY. You're hilarious.

BENJI. It's okay if I stay tonight, right?

KENNY. Oh...yeah. Um. Of course.

BENJI. It'll be a little embarrassing now. If I go home.

KENNY. No, I want you to stay. But my Dad will be here.

BENJI. Really?

KENNY. He's on his way right now.

BENJI. Right.

KENNY. But I want you to stay. You're staying. Yeah. And if he says something, I'll just tell him again: this is my house, right?

BENJI. Right. Your house. Yours and –

(*The sound of a car pulling up into the driveway.*)

KENNY. Oh, thank god.

(**KENNY** *runs offstage.* **BENJI** *waits, expectantly.*)

(**KENNY** *re-enters with* **EDITH** *who wears a cast on her right arm.* **BENJI** *claps the oven mitts together.*)

BENJI. Welcome home, Edith!

(**EDITH** *curtseys.*)

EDITH. Are you throwing me a party?

KENNY. A small one. You'll have a real one this weekend. I asked Dina Osheyack who to invite.

EDITH. They have to sign my cast. You have to sign my cast.

KENNY. We will.

BENJI. After dinner.

EDITH. What are you cooking?

KENNY. Chicken.

EDITH. Like Mom made?

KENNY. Yeah. Chicken afritada. Just for you, because we're so happy to have you back.

EDITH. I'm happy to be back. The hospital was better than the school, but I still didn't like it. Everyone was really nice, and I couldn't figure out why. I go, "I just broke my arm. You don't have to keep me here." And then I realized: they thought I tried to kill myself. So I said, "Why would I come all this way just to off myself? I'm trying to kill my dad!"

KENNY. You did not say that.

EDITH. No. Of course not.

KENNY. Did you?

EDITH. Yeah. Okay, yeah, I did. But then I laughed so they would think I was joking. But I saw his face. And he knows. Even though I'd never really do it, he knows that what I said was partly real.

He said he's going to stay here tonight.

KENNY. He said he'd probably stay through the weekend. He wants to make sure you're okay.

EDITH. He won't be here all the time now, will he?

KENNY. No, he won't. You know he won't.

EDITH. Good.

(*to* **BENJI**)

Is it a sleepover?

BENJI. Yeah.

EDITH. Good. Where's my gun?

(**KENNY** *and* **BENJI** *are quiet.*)

Did he throw it out?

KENNY. No.

BENJI. Why do you want it?

EDITH. Just give it to me.

(**KENNY** *exits.*)

BENJI. Where's your dad?

EDITH. In the car. I'm not going to shoot him.

BENJI. How do I know that?

EDITH. Because I'm telling you. I'm not going to shoot him.

BENJI. Don't shoot my mom, either.

EDITH. I won't.

(**KENNY** *returns with the gun.*)

KENNY. Don't shoot Dad.

EDITH. I'm not going to shoot Dad!

(**EDITH** *takes the gun. She holds it out to* **BENJI**.)

(**BENJI** *stares. She insists.* **BENJI** *takes the gun.*)

I can't fire it when my arm is in this thing. So you have to learn how to use it.

BENJI. Oh.

EDITH. You have to protect us now. I know you can do it.

BENJI. Okay.

EDITH. Will you take off those stupid mitts, you doofus? You can't shoot it with those mitts on.

(**BENJI** *puts the gun down, takes off the oven mitts, and then bends down hesitantly to pick it up again. Just before he can...*)

BANG! BANG!

(**BENJI** *jumps back.*)

BENJI. I don't really want to shoot it. I don't –

EDITH. Well, someone has to. Even when they take this thing off...I'm too young to be playing with firearms. You have to do it. Grown-ups have to do all kinds of things they may not want to do.

BENJI. Okay. Yes, ma'am.

(**BENJI** *picks up the gun.*)

EDITH. Good. We'll go in the back and shoot some pop cans after dinner. Thanks.

BENJI. You're welcome.

EDITH. You're going to learn how to take care of yourself. Even if you're not kicked out anymore I don't think you can count on your mom, Benji. Not all the time.

BENJI. I think you might be right.

KENNY. Why is Dad still in the car?

EDITH. He said he needed a minute.

KENNY. Go fetch him. Dinner's almost ready.

EDITH. Okay.

(**EDITH** *goes.*)

BENJI. She seems fine.

KENNY. Does she?

BENJI. Yeah. And she's going to teach me how to shoot.

KENNY. You don't have to.

BENJI. It's okay. It'll be fun. Besides, I have to learn to take care of myself.

KENNY. When we were in the hospital the other day. Me and Dad. He kept getting up – to get coffee or to call Chloë or to just go somewhere else. But I just planted myself and waited. And I watched him. I saw him. And he looked…so small. I mean, he's still taller than me, but he's not that much taller. Not anymore. And he just kept getting up, like he wanted to go – like he needed to. And I felt so bad for him.

I mean, Edith and I are here everyday. And things go wrong all the time. But all you have to do is take a little time, deal with a little stress, and then fix things. But it's like he made all these mistakes, and he just left them there. And they got bigger. And if he had taken care of them while they were small, maybe he would have realized it wasn't so bad, making mistakes. But now they were so big.

KENNY. *(cont.)* And I just felt so bad for him. He didn't know it was possible to just go home, and that there would be people there, and it would be okay. You could just fix it. And then you could feel good about it again. Even the part that was a mistake.

But why am I still scared, Benji?

BENJI. I don't think we'll ever stop being scared. I don't think we have to stop.

(BENJI holds KENNY. They kiss.)

(EDITH re-enters, shaken. KENNY sees her.)

KENNY. Ed?

EDITH. He's...

KENNY. What?

EDITH. Dad's in the car. He's crying. He said...he said to start dinner without him.

KENNY. Oh.

EDITH. He's just sitting there. Crying.

KENNY. Okay. Well...okay. We'll start dinner without him.

BENJI. I'll go set the table.

(BENJI exits.)

EDITH. Did I make him cry?

KENNY. I don't know.

EDITH. Should we wait?

KENNY. He said not to. He'll come in, eventually. Let's not wait. Let's just start without him.

(KENNY holds out a hand.)

Welcome home, Edith.

(EDITH gives him her hand. They exit to the kitchen.)

End of Scene

End of Act II

End of Play